MAY - - 2009

 W9-BBC-765

DISCARD

CHICAGO PUBLIC LIBRARY
BEVERLY BRANCH
1962 W. 95th STREET
CHICAGO, ILLINOIS 60643

The Alamo

CHICAGO PUBLIC LIBRARY
BEVERLY BRANCH
1962 W. 95th STREET
CHICAGO, ILLINOIS 60643

The Alamo

Dennis Brindell Fradin

Marshall Cavendish
Benchmark

New York

Acknowledgment

With special thanks to Richard Bruce Winders, Ph.D., historian and curator,

the Alamo, for his expert review of this manuscript.

Marshall Cavendish Benchmark
99 White Plains Road
Tarrytown, NY 10591
www.marshallcavendish.us

Text and map copyright © 2007 by Marshall Cavendish Corporation
Maps by XNR Productions

All rights reserved. No part of this book may be reproduced or utilized in any form or by
any means electronic or mechanical including photocopying, recording, or by any
information storage and retrieval system, without permission from the copyright holders.

All Internet sites were available and accurate when sent to press.

Library of Congress Cataloging-in-Publication Data

Fradin, Dennis B.
The Alamo / by Dennis Brindell Fradin.
p. cm. — (Turning points in U.S. history)
Includes bibliographical references and index.
ISBN-13: 978-0-7614-2127-6
ISBN-10: 0-7614-2127-0
1. Alamo (San Antonio, Tex.)—Juvenile literature. 2. Alamo (San Antonio, Tex.)—Siege, 1836—Juvenile literature. 3. Texas—History—
To 1846—Juvenile literature. 4. San Antonio (Tex.)—Buildings, structures, etc.—Juvenile literature. I. Title II. Series: Fradin, Dennis B.
Turning points of United States history.
F390.F79 2006
976.4'03—dc22
2005016022

Photo Research by Connie Gardner

Cover Photo: Royalty Free/CORBIS
Title page: Royalty Free/CORBIS
The photographs in this book are used by permission and through the courtesy of: *Corbis:* 6; David Muench, 10; Bettmann, 14, 20, 22, 30, 34; Craig
Aurness, 37; Sunset Bouleavrd/SYGMA, 43; *The Granger Collection:* 8, 16, 17, 32; *Getty Images:* Herbert Orth/Time Life Pictures, 9; Hulton Archive, 24-25, 26,
36, 40-41; *Institute of Texan Cultures at San Antonio:* 11, 28; *New York Public Library:* Art Resource, 13, 27; *Brown Brothers:* 19.

Editorial Director: Michelle Bisson
Art Director: Anahid Hamparian
Printed in China
1 3 5 6 4 2

R0429994791

Contents

Spanish missionaries walk out of the chapel for a religious ceremony in front of the Alamo, while Native Americans watch, some kneeling and praying.

CHAPTER ONE

"The Key to Texas"

Long before Texas became our twenty-eighth state, the flag of Spain flew over the region. Spain claimed Texas for three centuries starting in the early 1500s. The Spaniards built church settlements, called **missions**, where they taught the Indians about Christianity. They also built **presidios**, or forts, near the missions. The missions and forts marked the beginning of Goliad and several other Texas towns. For example, the Spaniards began San Antonio de Valero in 1718. This mission became known as the *Alamo*—Spanish for "cottonwood." It was the start of the city of San Antonio.

Spanish settlers moved to Texas. They came mostly from Mexico, a Spanish possession just south of Texas. Many of the settlers in Texas built cattle

ranches. Cowboys, called **vaqueros** in Spanish, tended the cattle. Yet, by 1800, only about four thousand Spanish settlers lived in Texas.

Meanwhile, in 1776, a new nation had been created—the United States of America. At first the nation consisted of the thirteen states on the East Coast, far to the east of Texas. But land-hungry American **pioneers** gradually fanned out westward.

The mission of San Xavier del Bac was founded in 1700.

Cowboys roping steer, from a painting by Charles Russell.

In 1820, an American named Moses Austin asked the Spanish government for permission to bring American settlers to Texas. Permission was granted, but conditions changed quickly. In 1821, Austin died. Also that year, Mexico broke away from Spanish rule and became independent. Mexico claimed Texas, and soon joined it together with the Mexican state of Coahuila as Coahuila y Tejas (Coahuila and Texas). Mexico's government allowed Austin's son, Stephen, to continue the project to settle Texas.

The Stephen F. Austin Memorial near Sealy, Texas.

G. T. T.

This engraving shows a man looking at a sign on a door that reads "G.T.T." Published in *Harper's New Monthly Magazine*, 1879.

Stephen F. Austin brought thousands of Americans to Texas during the 1820s. A big reason Texas attracted settlers was that land was twelve and a half cents an **acre** there—compared to a dollar and a quarter an acre for public land in the United States. The Americans built farms where they grew cotton and began such towns as Washington-on-the-Brazos, Columbus, and San Felipe. Many Americans with "Texas fever" simply wrote **G.T.T.** (Gone to Texas) on the doors of their homes in the United States and headed to this region that belonged to Mexico. Because he brought in six thousand settlers in ten years, Stephen Austin became known as the "Father of Texas."

Mexican officials hadn't minded some Americans settling in Texas. But with so many Americans heading there, Mexican officials were afraid the newcomers would take over the region. In 1830 Mexico passed a law to halt American **immigration** to Texas. The Americans kept coming anyway.

By the mid-1830s, the vast majority of the 30,000 settlers in Texas were from the United States. They resented the immigration policies and taxes imposed by Mexico and were beginning to think that perhaps Texas should be part of the United States.

In 1835, Texans began a war to break free from Mexican rule. The first battle was fought on October 2, 1835, at Gonzales, near San Antonio, where Texas farmers defeated a Mexican force. A week later, the Texans captured Goliad. Encouraged by their successes, the rebels advanced on San Antonio and captured it in December 1835.

Mexico's ruler, Antonio Lopez de Santa Anna, was determined

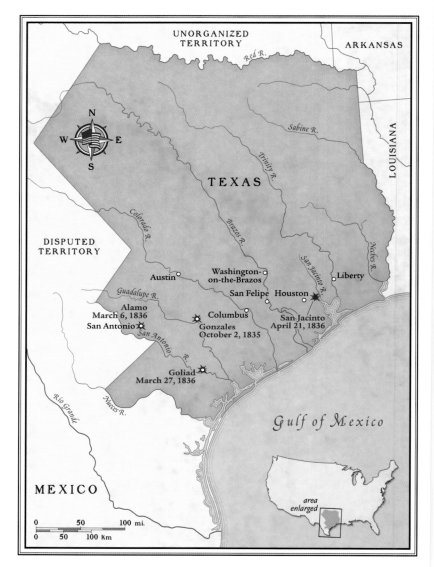

Battle Sites

This painting depicts the surrender of General Santa Anna after the Battle of San Jacinto, April 22, 1836.

to crush the revolt. He raised an army in Mexico to fight the rebels. General Santa Anna marched his men toward San Antonio, where a group of rebels had taken refuge at the fortified mission called the Alamo. One American considered it so important to defend the Alamo from the approaching Mexican army that he called the fort "the key to Texas."

This undated engraving shows James Bowie fighting with Indians.

CHAPTER TWO

"Victory or Death"

By Valentine's Day—February 14, 1836—about 150 rebels had gathered at the Alamo. That day, two of its defenders agreed to share the command. One was James Bowie, a Kentucky native who had lived in San Antonio for several years. Bowie was a rugged Indian fighter and slave trader. He was said to have invented a hunting knife and weapon with a curved blade that was named the bowie knife—after him. He was determined to defend the Alamo and would "rather die in these ditches than give it up to the enemy," he wrote in a letter.

His **cocommander** at the Alamo was William Barret Travis, a South Carolina-born lawyer who had come to Texas in 1831 and had opened a law

office in San Felipe. Travis, who was only twenty-six years old, was a moody, thoughtful man who liked to read. A leader of the Texas **independence** movement, he declared in a letter written from the Alamo on February 13: "It is more important to occupy this post than I imagined. It is the key to Texas."

William Barret Travis was the commander at the siege of the Alamo.

Vol. 2.] "GO AHEAD!!" [No. 3.

THE CROCKETT ALMANAC 1841.

Tussel with a Bear. See page 9.

**Containing Adventures, Exploits, Sprees
& Scrapes in the West, &
Life and Manners in the Backwoods.**

Nashville, Tennessee. Published by Ben Harding.

Davy Crockett, with the help of his dog, is shown fighting a bear on the cover of *The Crockett Almanac*, 1841.

Later, thirty-two more **volunteers** arrived from Gonzales, swelling the number of the Alamo's defenders to about two hundred. Besides Bowie and Travis, the best-known of the rebels included Davy Crockett, a hunter and lawmaker from Tennessee whose motto was: "Be always sure you're right— then go ahead!"

In fact, Tennessee had been the birthplace of at least thirty of the men at the Alamo, the most of any state. They included three brothers: Edward, James, and George Taylor, who had come to live in Liberty, Texas. About ten defenders were **Tejanos**. These were people of Mexican ancestry who had been born in Texas or moved there. About thirty of the

General Santa Anna

After his capture at the Battle of San Jacinto, General Santa Anna was released. He later ruled Mexico again. While on a visit to New York City in 1867, Santa Anna was seen chewing a substance that came from trees. This was said to have helped inspire the establishment of America's chewing gum industry.

approximately two hundred men at the Alamo were foreign-born. Eleven hailed from England, nine from Ireland, four from Scotland, two from Germany, and one each from Wales and Denmark. The birthplaces of a number of defenders are unknown.

On February 23, 1836, General Santa Anna's army approached the Alamo. The Mexican army had about 2,500 men, which meant it outnumbered the rebels by more than ten to one. Nonetheless, the rebels had some advantages. By 1836 the Alamo was much more than a church. It was a three-acre complex bordered by protective walls and buildings.

The two sides began firing at each other. Day after day the Mexican army and the rebels exchanged cannon fire and gunshots. Within the Alamo complex the enemy bombardment tore up the ground until it resembled the craters of the moon. Yet, amazingly, a week passed and not one rebel was killed or wounded.

The situation was deteriorating at the Alamo, though. Commander Bowie was very ill and couldn't stir from his cot, leaving his cocommander, Colonel Travis, in charge. Travis repeatedly wrote messages asking for aid, which he sent out by **courier** from the Alamo. One message declared: "I shall never surrender or retreat. I call on you in the name of Liberty, of patriotism, & everything dear to the American character, to come to our aid, with all dispatch. VICTORY OR DEATH." But, except for the thirty-two volunteers from Gonzales, no reinforcements reached the Alamo in time.

Day after day, the slaughter at the Alamo went on.

Colonel William Travis watches as his troops cross the line and choose to fight.

By March 5 the Alamo's walls were crumbling from being pounded by Mexican cannon fire. That day Colonel Travis summoned the Alamo's two hundred defenders to the plaza within the complex, where he spoke to them plainly: "My brave companions," he reportedly said, "our fate is sealed. Within a few days—perhaps a very few hours—we must all be in eternity. This is our certain doom." Travis added that they might try to surrender or escape over the walls, but that, as for himself, he would stay and fight to his last breath. According to some accounts, he then took his sword and carved a long line in the dirt. Everyone who chose to remain and fight, he said, should cross the line.

Every man except one crossed the line. The lone exception climbed over the wall, escaped, and lived to tell the story.

THE LAST STAND AT THE ALAMO

The flag that floated over the ill-fated mission fortress The Alamo, at San Antonio, in 1836, was that of the Republic of Texas, then fighting for the right to self-government. Its design was that of the Mexican flag, with the eagle, serpent and cactus replaced by the date 1824. This indicated adherence to the Texas constitution of that date, overthrown by Santa Anna, who established a dictatorship. Besieged by 4,000 troops under Santa Anna, the little garrison of 183 Americans held out 12 days under constant bombardment.

1824

From the flat roof with its thick adobe walls, the Texan sharpshooters directed a devastating fire in the defense described in the diary left by Davy Crockett, famed scout, hunter and Indian fighter whose career ended here. Finally the defenders were so weakened that, after two unsuccessful assaults, an entrance was made through sheer weight of numbers and the five lone survivors were slain. The slogan "Remember the Alamo" became a battle-cry which led to Santa Anna's destruction and the ultimate victory of the Texans.

THE ALAMO FLAG

The last stand at the Alamo is pictured in this undated lithograph.

CHAPTER THREE

"Come on, Boys!"

Meanwhile, General Santa Anna and his officers had been talking to their men, too. They had a very different point of view than the Alamo's defenders. Texas was part of Mexico, they pointed out. The Americans were armed rebels who were trying to seize Mexican territory, after Mexico had been so kind as to let them settle there. Because of all this, the rebel army at the Alamo deserved to be destroyed.

On the night of March 5, 1836, the nearly full moon rose over the Alamo behind a bank of clouds. That Saturday night General Santa Anna had his men prepare for a final assault.

The Texan defenders of the Alamo fighting Mexican soldiers within the walls of the Alamo. Davy Crockett is center left, holding his rifle above his head.

Davy Crockett

Davy Crockett was known for his tall tales, and other people also told them about him. It was said that Crockett rode alligators for exercise and once made a bear retreat by grinning at it. Because of all the legends about Crockett, people sometimes forget that he was a real man who served in the Tennessee legislature and in the U.S. House of Representatives before he went to Texas. The Davy Crockett Cabin, where he once lived, can be visited in Rutherford, Tennessee.

The final assault on the Alamo.

Before dawn on Sunday, March 6, the sound of a bugle came from the Mexican army. A lookout at the Alamo saw a huge number of soldiers advancing and yelled out, "The Mexicans are coming!"

The commotion awoke the rebels, who headed to the walls. "Come on, boys," Colonel William Travis called to his men, "the Mexicans are upon us, and we'll give them hell!"

From their positions along the wall, the Americans shot at the onrushing army. The Mexican troops fell by the hundreds, some brought down by the American marksmen, others accidentally shot by their fellow soldiers in the dim morning light. Although

The death of Davy Crockett at the Alamo.

suffering huge losses, the Mexican army moved closer and closer. They placed ladders against the walls and soon were inside the Alamo complex. For the next few minutes the two sides fought furiously with guns and swords. Colonel Travis was reportedly killed while firing his shotgun at the enemy. According to one report, James Bowie was firing his guns from his cot when he was shot to death. It was said that Davy Crockett and five other men were taken prisoner, but then executed by order of General Santa Anna.

By eight o'clock in the morning, the Battle of the Alamo was over. The Mexicans had wiped out the defenders of the Alamo, but had suffered enormous **casualties** themselves. Estimates vary but perhaps as many as six hundred of

Suzanna A. Dickinson was one of the few survivors of the battle at the Alamo.

General Santa Anna's troops had been killed or wounded. Although all of the approximately two hundred rebel fighters were dead, about twenty **noncombatants** had been spared. They included women, children, and Colonel Travis's slave, Joe. Much of what we know about the Battle of the Alamo comes from information provided by the survivors.

This note for twenty dollars was issued by the Treasury Department of the Government of Texas in Houston, April 1838.

General Houston looked for a chance to strike a crushing blow at the Mexican army. It came on April 21, 1836, along the San Jacinto River in southeast Texas. Near where the city of Houston now stands, about 900 men under Sam Houston's command prepared to fight General Santa Anna's 1,400 troops.

"Victory is certain!" Houston told his men. "Trust in God and fear not! And remember the Alamo!"

The Battle of San Jacinto turned into a bloodbath. Shouting "Remember the Alamo! Remember Goliad!" the Texans killed hundreds of Mexican soldiers who tried to surrender. Only about nine Texas troops were killed compared to about 630 Mexican **fatalities**. General Santa Anna himself was among the 730 Mexicans taken prisoner.

The Republic of Texas

President Anson Jones of Texas declares an end to the Republic of Texas and the joining of Texas as a new state in the United States of America.

The Texans' victory at San Jacinto ended the revolution. Texas had won its independence. For about ten years, Texas was an independent country called the Republic of Texas. Sam Houston became the republic's first president. The republic issued its own money and had its own flag. But most Texans wanted the Republic of Texas to join the United States. On December 29, 1845, Texas was admitted to the Union as our twenty-eighth state.

Sam Houston

Sam Houston, who was born in Virginia, ran away from home when he was about fifteen. He went to live with the Cherokee Indians, who adopted him into their tribe and nicknamed him "the Raven." He later served as governor of Tennessee from 1827 to 1829 but after his wife left him he resigned and moved back with the Cherokees. By 1835 he had settled permanently in Texas, where he commanded the Texas army that defeated Santa Anna and was elected president of the Republic of Texas. After that, he served as a U.S. senator and then governor of the Lone Star State.

General Zachary Taylor leads the U.S. troops into the Battle of Palo Alto during the Mexican-American War.

Mexico still felt that Texas had been taken from it unjustly. This contributed to the outbreak of war between the United States and Mexico in 1846. A far more powerful country than Mexico, the United States won what it called the Mexican War in 1848. As a result, the United States received a huge amount of what had been Mexican land, including all or parts of California, Nevada, Utah, Arizona, Wyoming, Colorado, and New Mexico.

To this day the fight at the Alamo is the best-known event in Texas history and the phrase "Remember the Alamo" stirs strong feelings. It reminds us that Mexico once ruled Texas and other parts of what is now the United States. And it reminds us of a brave group of men who lost a battle but helped build a nation.

The San Jacinto Monument marks the site of the battle of the Alamo.

Glossary

acre—A unit of land equal to 43,560 square feet; an acre that is square-shaped and measures about 209 feet on each of its four sides.

Alamo—A fortified mission in Texas where a famous battle was fought on March 6, 1836.

casualties—People killed or wounded in a war or another disaster.

cocommanders—Two or more people who share leadership.

courier—Messenger.

fatalities—Deaths.

immigration—The act of moving to a different country to live.

independence—Freedom, or self-government.

massacre—The large-scale killing of people who cannot defend themselves.

missions—Settlements that developed around a church.

noncombatants—People in a wartime situation who are not involved in the fighting.

pioneers—People who are among the first to move into a region.

presidios—Spanish forts.

Tejanos—People of Mexican ancestry who were born in Texas or had moved there.

vaqueros—Cowboys.

volunteers—People who come forward to help of their own free will, rather than those forced to serve.

Timeline

1519—Spaniard Alonso Alvarez de Pineda makes the first known exploration of Texas

1682—First two Spanish missions are built in Texas

1718—The Spanish mission that became known as the Alamo is founded

1776—United States of America declares its independence

1820—Moses Austin plans an American colony in Texas but dies the next year

1821—Mexico gains independence from Spain and takes control of Texas; Moses' son Stephen F. Austin establishes first American settlements in Texas

1830—Mexico passes a law to halt American immigration to Texas, but people from the United States keep settling the region

mid-1830s—Texas has about 30,000 settlers, the majority of them from the United States

1835—The war for Texan independence begins on October 2

1519　　　　　　　*1821*　　*1835*

1836—February 23: General Santa Anna's army approaches the Alamo

March 2: Texas declares its independence

March 6: The Alamo falls

April 21: Sam Houston's Texas army defeats General Santa Anna at the Battle of San Jacinto; Texas has won its independence

1836–1845—Texas is the independent Republic of Texas

1845—On December 29, Texas becomes our twenty-eighth state

1846–1848—United States defeats Mexico in the Mexican War and takes a vast tract of land now comprising all or part of seven states from Mexico in exchange for $15 million

1986—Hundred and fiftieth anniversary of the Battle of the Alamo

1836   *1845*   *1986*

Further Information

BOOKS

Carter, Alden R. *Last Stand at the Alamo*. New York: Franklin Watts, 1990.

Lace, William W. *The Alamo*. San Diego: Lucent, 1998.

Murphy, Jim. *Inside the Alamo*. New York: Delacorte, 2003.

WEB SITE

Web site home page for the Alamo:
http://www.thealamo.org

F I L M   A N D   T E L E V I S I O N

Many films and television shows have been made about the Alamo and Davy Crockett. This is just a small selection.

The Alamo, 2004.

Alamo: The Price of Freedom, 1988.

The Alamo: Thirteen Days to Glory, 1987 (TV).

The Alamo, starring John Wayne, 1960 (nominated for Best Picture Oscar award).

John Wayne and Linda Cristal filming *The Alamo*.

Bibliography

Davis, William C. *Three Roads to the Alamo: The Lives and Fortunes of David Crockett, James Bowie, and William Barret Travis*. New York: HarperCollins, 1998.

Long, Jeff. *Duel of Eagles: The Mexican and U.S. Fight for the Alamo*. New York: Morrow, 1990.

Lord, Walter. *A Time to Stand: The Epic of the Alamo*. Lincoln: University of Nebraska Press, 1978 (reprint of 1961 edition).

Roberts, Randy, and James S. Olson. *A Line in the Sand: The Alamo in Blood and Memory*. New York: Free Press, 2001.

Winders, Richard Bruce. *Crisis in the Southwest: The United States, Mexico, and the Struggle over Texas*. Wilmington, Delaware: Scholarly Resources, 2002.

Index

Page numbers in **boldface** are illustrations.

About the Author

Dennis Fradin is the author of 150 books, some of them written with his wife, Judith Bloom Fradin. Their recent book for Clarion, *The Power of One: Daisy Bates and the Little Rock Nine*, was named a Golden Kite Honor Book. Another of Dennis's recent books is *Let It Begin Here! Lexington & Concord: First Battles of the American Revolution*, published by Walker. The Fradins are currently writing a biography of social worker and anti-war activist Jane Addams for Clarion and a nonfiction book about a slave escape for National Geographic Children's Books. Turning Points in U.S. History is Dennis Fradin's first series for Marshall Cavendish Benchmark. The Fradins have three grown children and three young grandchildren.